VOLUNTEER BULLET

by

CARL MARTIN

•

SWORD OF THE KING

by

CARL MARTIN

RL 2.0-3.5

Developed by Cebulash Associates
Design by Square Moon Productions
Cover Photo by Richard Hutchings

1-55855-690-7

VOLUNTEER BULLET

BY

CARL MARTIN

Willie Tarbell was big. He stood well over 6 feet and was almost too wide to walk around. That made him just right for playing on a football team, and that is what he did. He played for the Buffalo Bullets. When he was all suited up in the team's black and green colors, he was as big as any player could hope to be.

His friend, Peter Costa, was only 5 foot 7 and maybe 135 if he had his pockets filled with stones. But he was on the Bullets, too. Not because he was big—he wasn't—but because he could send a football to the moon if he put his foot into it.

Now as the two of them walked in Delaware Park, they looked strange together.

They weren't anything alike. But they both loved the game of football.

That was why they were in the park, even though it was weeks before the Bullets would be playing again. Whenever they had a little time, they would go to the park and pass the ball around. Sometimes they would run side by side around the park, but most of the time they just played catch, passing a football to each other.

Willie was in the middle of the field, passing the ball to Pete, who was on the north side of the field. There were about 200 feet between them, but that was no problem for Willie. He had a good arm.

It was Pete who had a little trouble. When he passed the ball back, sometimes it didn't go all the way to Willie. It almost always hit the ground 30 feet in front of him. Then Willie had to walk to get it.

They had been playing for 15 minutes when Pete missed Willie with a short pass. Only this time it didn't hit the ground in front of Willie. Some man in gray work clothes ran in from the left, reached up, and caught the ball. He was wearing heavy work shoes, too, but he didn't let them slow him down.

"Good catch!" Willie called. Then he held his hands out so the man would pass the ball to him. But the man didn't do it. He just stood there with a smile on his face.

"Pass the ball," Willie said, walking toward him.

"This is a nice ball," the man said. "It has a nice feel to it."

"Thanks," Willie said. Then he added, "Pass it here."

"No, I don't think so," the man said. "I think I'll keep it."

"Pass it here," Willie said in a hard voice.

The man shook his head no. "I'm going to keep it," he said.

"Don't fool around," Willie said and moved toward him.

The man stood his ground until Willie made a grab for the ball. Then he turned quickly and ran off with the ball under his left arm.

Willie didn't know what to do. He could not believe this was happening. Then he saw the man was heading toward Pete Costa. "Stop him, Pete," he called.

Pete must have heard him because he moved to stand in the man's path.

The man saw him, but he didn't slow down or turn. But when he got near Pete, he picked up speed and ran all the faster. Pete made a grab for him, but all he got for his trouble was a hand full of air. The man went past like a shot and quickly lost himself in the park.

Willie and Pete stood with their mouths open until he was gone.

2

Willie began to laugh. Then Pete started. And that made Willie laugh so hard he had to sit on the grass. If any people had picked that time to walk past, they would have thought the big man was crazy or something.

Suddenly Pete was quiet. "What are we laughing at?" he wanted to know. "That was a $30 ball he just ran off with."

"Yes, I know," Willie said, still laughing. "Do you think he knew who we are?"

"What are you trying to say?"

"Do you think he knew we play for the Bullets?" Willie asked.

Pete thought for a minute. Then he made a face. "I sure hope not," he said. "It is bad enough that we had our ball taken from us. It would be even worse if he knew we are Bullets and told people. I would feel like a fool, wouldn't you?"

"Come to think of it, I guess I would," Willie said.

"I think we should do something about it," Pete said.

"Sure, but what? The man was a stranger. I never saw him before. Did you?"

"No, never," Pete said, as he took a seat on the grass beside Willie. "I just think we should get our ball back."

"So, what makes you think we can find him again?"

"I don't know if we can. I only know we should see if we can."

"Sure, but how are we going to do that? Where do we start looking?"

"Right here in the park," Pete said. "If he knows we are Bullets, he may never come back. But if he does not know, he probably will show up again. Maybe he works near here, or takes a shortcut past here every day. We can spend more time in the park and watch for him."

Willie got to his feet and helped Pete up. "It does not sound as though we have much chance of catching the man," he said. "But I guess there isn't anything else we can do."

So they went to Delaware Park as much as they could for the next three weeks—they walked there, ran there, and passed their new football there. They started out thinking they might have good luck. But at the end of the three weeks, they didn't have much hope of seeing the man again.

"Well, we can be happy no one found out we lost our ball," Willie said.

"We had it taken from us, remember?" Pete said.

"OK—*taken*," Willie said, but he didn't sound happy about it. "Let's not talk about it anymore. It is all over and there's nothing we can do about it."

The big man started to walk away. "Go out for a pass," he told Pete. "We still have time for a few more."

Pete ran to the end of the field and waited. Willie brought his arm back and pointed the ball toward the sky.

Then he heard Pete shout his name and looked over to see him jumping up and down. Pete wanted Willie to look at something behind him. Before he could turn, the man in the gray work clothes ran up and took the ball out of his hand. The man looked back, smiled once, and then raced away into the park.

Pete ran up to Willie. "He did it again," he said.

"No fooling, Dick Tracy. How did you work that out?" Willie said.

"That man sure can run," Pete said.

"I saw," Willie said.

"I never saw anyone run that fast. And he was wearing heavy work shoes," Pete said. "I don't think I'll ever forget that."

Willie walked over to a soft drink can at the side of the field and gave it a kick. "There is something I'll never forget, too," he said.

"What is that?" Pete wanted to know.

"The man's smile," Willie said.

3

The next day the Bullets began getting ready for their game with the Cleveland Outlaws. From then on, Willie and Pete didn't have much time to think about the man who ran off with their footballs. They were too busy getting ready to face the Outlaws. They had played against the Outlaws two times the year before and lost both times. They didn't want that to happen again.

But that was what was going to happen. Almost everyone was sure of it. The Bullets were a good team, but the Outlaws were better. They had too many men on their team who could catch the ball and then move down the field like rockets. The Bullets didn't have even one man who could do that.

"What we need," Pete said, "is to find the man who took our footballs."

"Forget that," Willie said. "Even if we could find him, we could not catch him."

Willie was big, but he wasn't as smart as Pete. He didn't know that Pete had a plan.

"And no one else could," Pete said.

Willie looked lost. "What are you saying?"

"I'm saying, he is a man we could use on our team. The Bullets need a man who can run like he can. Just think—he can go like a rocket even wearing work shoes. Can you guess how fast he would be if he had the right shoes?"

"Faster?"

"Not just faster—much faster!" Pete said.

"All right, say we do find him. He will probably just run away from us again. He has done that two times now," Willie pointed out.

"We will have to make sure he does not get away," Pete said.

"How?" asked Willie.

"We will have to catch up with him in a place where he can't run away," Pete said.

4

"I think he works around here somewhere," Pete said. It was their day off, and he and Willie were in Delaware Park again. It seemed to them they were spending more time in the park than at home.

"Why do you say that?" Willie said.

"Because this is the only place we have seen him. And I don't think he knows we're Bullets. Even a man who is that fast would think a while before he took a football away from a Buffalo Bullet."

"OK, I'll buy that," Willie told Pete. "But where could he work? There is nothing around here."

"There is one place," Pete said, pointing to a roof that could be seen from all over the park.

"That must be the zoo," Willie said.

"Right," Pete said. "Let's take a walk over there and look around."

As soon as they got to the zoo, they knew it was the right place. Everywhere they looked there seemed to be one or two men in gray work clothes and heavy work shoes. They were the men who took care of the animals.

Now if they could just find out where the man with the sticky fingers worked, their troubles would be over—maybe.

Each kind of animal had a building all to itself. They started walking around inside the buildings, one by one. They wanted to get a look at the men working there without being seen. That took time. Sometimes they had to wait many minutes for a man to turn around so they could see his face. Other times they had to wait for a man to come nearer. There was no way they could hurry it, so they had covered only half the buildings when the zoo bell rang, telling everyone to leave. It was time to quit work.

"Now what?" Willie said.

Pete spoke to a man in gray work clothes as he walked past them. "Tell me," Pete asked, "what gate do you men use at night?"

"Over there," the man said, pointing. "The one by the parking spaces."

"Thanks," Pete said, and the man went on his way.

Pete and Willie walked out the gate and stood by a fence. From there they could see everyone who left the zoo, but they could not be seen. Ten minutes later, they saw their man. Even in his heavy shoes he seemed so light-footed he might have been walking on air.

"There he is!" Willie said, and he took a step toward the man.

Pete took his arm. "Not so fast. If we try to talk to him out here, he will just run away from us again. You know we can't catch him. I don't think anyone could."

"You are right," Willie said. "So what should we do?"

"Just wait a minute," Pete said.

They watched the man walk to a beat-up old car and get in. As he drove away, Pete went to the gate. A few of the workers were standing there talking.

"Do you know that man who just left?" Pete asked. "The one who walks like a dancer."

"Sure, we know him. That was Bill Smith," one of the men said.

"Do you know where he works?"

"The bird house," the man answered.

5

"Now what do we do?" Willie wanted to know.

"We have to wait until we can catch him inside the bird house. He will have no place to run and we can talk to him there."

"But we're going to Cleveland in the morning to play the Outlaws. We won't be back in Buffalo for days."

"What are you worrying about? Do you think he will get sick and die on us?"

"No. I just wish we had been able to grab him now. I don't like waiting. Anything can happen when you wait."

"That is what I like about you, Willie—you always look on the bright side of things."

The game against the Outlaws went just the way everyone had thought it would. The Outlaws beat the Bullets 42 to 6, and it was Pete's foot that had earned the 6 points for the Bullets. The Bullets could not seem to move the ball down the field. If Pete had not been able to kick like an angry horse, the Outlaws would have had a shutout.

After the game, Pete told the team's owner that he and Willie knew a man who might be just right for the team. "He is very fast," Pete said.

"But does he have sticky fingers?" the owner asked.

"Sticky fingers? Are you asking if he takes things?"

"No, I'm asking if he can hold on to the ball."

"Well," Pete said, "once he gets his hands on one, he does not like to let it go. I can tell you that."

"Good. Bring the man around. I would like to see him," the owner said.

Pete and Willie sat next to each other on the trip back to Buffalo.

"I wish you had not said anything to the owner," Willie said.

"Why not?"

Willie made a face. "I don't know. It does not seem right—like it might be bad luck."

"Bad luck?" Pete said as though he could not believe what he was hearing.

"You know—something could go wrong," Willie said.

"What could go wrong?"

"I don't know—something."

"The only bad thing that could happen is that the man would tell everyone how he took footballs away from us," Pete said.

"If he brings that up, I'll kill him," Willie said, punching the seat in front of him.

Willie and Pete had to spend the day after they got back to Buffalo with the team. They sat watching movies of the game against the Outlaws all day. It was bad enough to have lost the game. But it was worse to sit and watch every bad play two or three times. Every minute they watched the movies seemed like a year.

When they were finally able to leave, they headed for the zoo and the bird house.

"How are we going to work this?" Willie said. "We can't let him run away from us again."

"Right," Pete said. "Tell you what—when we get inside, you wait at the door. If he should try to get away again, you can grab him. I'll go inside and try to talk to him."

"OK. That sounds like the smart way to do it," Willie said.

So when they went inside, Willie stayed by the door and waited—and waited—and waited.

At last Pete returned alone. "You were right," he said. "Talking to the owner *was* bad luck."

"What happened?" Willie asked. "Don't tell me he never heard of the Bullets!"

"Worse than that," Pete said. "He isn't

here. Doesn't work here anymore. The day we saw him was his last day on the job. They think he left the city, and no one knows where we can find him."

6

Willie and Pete stayed up most of the night. They kept trying to think of some way they could find the man. But they could not think of a good plan. They could not even think of a bad one. There didn't seem to be any way to find the man.

"If only we had gone to the zoo before that last day," Willie said. "We could have talked to him before he left the city."

"And if the Bullets had more good players, we wouldn't need him," Pete added.

The following day Pete and Willie ran some new plays with the team. Every once in a while, Pete or Willie would ask the other if he had thought of anything. The answer was always no.

They couldn't seem to think of anything else, and it showed. Willie missed the ball even when it should have been easy to catch. And when it was Pete's turn to kick, he didn't do as well as he used to.

"What is wrong with you two?" the owner asked. "Can't you keep your minds on the game?"

They didn't say anything.

"And where is that man you said you were going to bring around? I hope he plays better than you do."

There was nothing they could say, so they kept their mouths shut.

True, Pete had learned the man's name from the people at the zoo, but that didn't help much. There had to be 50 men named Bill Smith in every large city. They could spend the rest of their lives talking to men named Bill Smith and never find the right one. There didn't seem to be a chance in the world that they would ever find the man.

"Why didn't he just keep his sticky fingers off our footballs?" Willie said.

"Right. Then things would be better," Pete said.

"There is one good thing though," Willie added.

"What?"

"If he has left the city, we won't have to worry that he will take our ball the next time we go to the park," Willie said.

"Say," Pete said. "Maybe you are on to something. You said, 'If he has left.' We don't know that he has. We only know that the men at the zoo thought he was going to leave. But we don't know that he did."

"You think there is a chance that he didn't?"

"Sure. There's always a chance," Pete said.

"And if he is still in the city, maybe he will come to the park again?"

"Maybe," Pete said with a nod.

Willie smiled for the first time that day. "Now I don't feel so bad," he said. "We have something to hope for."

"But not much," Pete said. "We're back where we started. If we do see him again, how are we going to get him to stay and talk to us? He must think we're angry about the footballs he took from us."

"I didn't think of that," Willie said.

They both thought about it the rest of the afternoon. Even after they had changed into their street clothes, they didn't have an answer to the problem.

"Want to look around the park right now?" Willie asked.

"Sure, let's take a look," Pete said.

Suddenly, Willie's name was called: "Willie! Willie Tarbell!"

It was the owner, standing in the doorway.

"Now what?" Willie said in a low voice only Pete could hear. He walked over. "Yes?" he said.

"The mailman left something for you in the office," the owner said. "Pick it up on your way out."

Willie told Pete he had to pick up some mail, and the two of them went to the office together. But it wasn't a letter—it was a large box.

Willie opened it, and out fell their missing footballs. While Willie looked at the footballs with wide eyes, Pete looked at the box. In the corner was the name Bill Smith and the place where he lived.

7

"The note that he sent with the footballs—what did it say?" Pete asked. They were in his car, heading for Bill Smith's house. He lived near Delaware Park.

"He said it had all been a joke and he hoped we didn't have any hard feelings."

"Is that all?"

"What more do you want?" Willie asked. "Now we know where he lives, don't we?"

"Sure," Pete said. Then he added, "If he has not moved."

"Why did you have to say that?" Willie asked.

"I guess I'm getting used to bad luck," Pete said.

"I don't want to get used to it," Willie said.

Smith lived in an old house on Elmwood Street. Pete parked in the driveway and they climbed out. They found Bill Smith in the back, working on the grass.

"We want to talk to you," Willie called.

Smith looked up, then from left to right as though trying to find a way to escape.

"We're not mad," Pete added quickly.

Smith quit looking for a way out.

Pete got right to the point. "Would you like to try out for the Bullets?" he asked.

"Do birds fly?" Bill Smith answered.

8

Willie and Pete took Bill with them the next morning. They got him suited up and even found shoes that he could wear. "Now you look like a football player," Pete said.

"Thanks," Smith answered.

"But we have to get something straight before we go onto the field," Willie said.

"What is it?" Smith asked.

The big man took Smith by the arm. "If you ever tell anyone you took those footballs away from us, I'll break both your legs," Willie said.

"And I'll help him," Pete said.

"OK. I'll never tell," Bill Smith said.

"Then let's go outside." Pete led the way and took him to where the owner was standing. "This is the man I was telling you about," he said.

The owner looked Smith over and seemed to like what he saw. "Let's see what you can do," he said.

He sent Bill out for a pass. The ball came in high. It looked like Bill would miss it, but he jumped up, reached out, and pulled it to him with one hand. Then he ran to the end of the field like he was on fire. No one could catch him. No one could even put a hand on him.

"Let's see if he can do that again," the owner said.

The next time Smith did even better. He pulled in a pass that was as bad as the first one and ran faster than he had before.

"That man *does* have sticky fingers," the owner said.

"I told you so," Pete said.

"And he *is* fast," the owner said. "He is as fast as . . . as fast as . . . " He was working to find the right word.

Willie spoke up. "He is as fast as a Bullet," he said.

The owner smiled. "Right—he is as fast as a Bullet."

The Bullets lost their next two games. Bill Smith didn't play. He had to learn many things before he could play in a real game with the rest of the team. But he learned quickly. When he did play, he didn't do anything wrong.

When the Bullets played the Outlaws again later in the year, Bill Smith had one of his best days. The Bullets beat the Outlaws 35 to 7. It was a home game.

Willie came up to Bill when it was over and hit him on the arm. "Good game!" he said.

"Thanks."

"Pete and I are going to the park on our day off to pass a ball around."

"Is it OK if I come, too?"

"Only if you don't run off with the ball," Willie said.

SWORD OF THE KING

CARL MARTIN

Rita Green got to the racetrack at four o'clock in the morning, just as she always did. Rita parked outside and walked to the gate. The man at the gate waved to her as she walked past.

The sun wasn't up, but a few people were. Some men were cleaning stalls. Others were helping the horses get ready for their morning run. The rest of the track was dark and quiet, but around the stables the workday had started.

Rita had had a few other jobs, but she liked to work outdoors in the cool air better than anything else. She liked the smell of the stables. Most of all, she liked the horses. It made her feel good to be around them.

Each morning she jumped out of bed right away. She could not get to work soon enough. She had a good thing and she knew it. Not everyone was paid to take care of a great racehorse like Sword of the King.

She went into the new stable building. That is where Sword of the King had his stall. She walked down the wide center aisle to the horse's stall and stopped in front of its two-piece door. The top part or the lower part could be opened by itself while the other half was left shut.

She opened the lower half and Sparky the dog danced out. He must have heard the sound of Rita's footsteps.

When Rita first learned that a little black dog lived in Sword of the King's stall, she didn't know what to make of it. It didn't sound very safe for the dog. Then she learned there was no danger from the big horse. "Why is that?" Rita had asked Mr. Boynton, Sword of the King's owner.

"Because the horse loves that little dog," Mr. Boynton had said.

"No fooling?"

"No fooling," Mr. Boynton had said.

Now Rita reached inside the stall and got the piece of rope she used when she took Sparky for his morning walk. She tied it around the dog and left the stable with Sparky at her side.

The little dog jumped around almost as much as the horses did that early in the morning. They seemed to like being up while it was still dark outside. Rita thought that was strange. People did not act like that very often, but the animals always seemed to.

She took the dog to an open field near the track and took off the rope. Sparky ran into the dark and was gone.

Rita gave the dog a few minutes. Then she put her hand to her mouth and made a sound to call him back. Sparky showed up as quickly as he had left.

Rita tied the dog with the rope again. When she looked up, two men were standing in front of her.

Just like that—suddenly, there they were. They had made no noise. And with the lights from one of the stables behind them, she could not see their faces.

2

Rita felt cold fear run up her back. Then one of the men spoke—the thin one. "Hello, Rita," he said. "Walking the dog again?"

Suddenly, Rita knew who they were and felt better.

The men, Mike and Harry, had been around the stables for the past two weeks.

They wanted to learn which were the best horses. Then they would bet on those horses and make money—they thought!

"Yes, I walk him two or three times a day," Rita answered. "He is a nice little dog."

"You like him?" Mike, the thin one, asked.

"Sure. I said he's a nice little dog. Never any trouble."

"What about Sword of the King?" Harry, the heavy one, asked. "Do you still think he's the best horse in the big race on Monday?"

"I sure do," Rita said. "Just about everyone will be backing him."

"Good . . . good," Mike said. Then they turned and walked away with quiet steps.

Rita thought that all the people who bet on horse races were pretty strange, so she didn't think too much about it. She did wonder how they got back to the stables. There were men at all the gates to make sure no one went there without a stable pass. She did not think Mike and Harry belonged back there, but they must have. How else could they be there?

The sky was almost light by the time Rita and Sparky got back to the stable. She let the dog into Sword of the King's stall. Sparky went right to his bed in the corner and rolled up into a black ball. The big horse put his head down to touch noses with Sparky. Then he let Rita know he was ready for his breakfast.

Rita had to work until early afternoon. Then she was finished for the day. Before she left, she took Sparky for a walk down by the track.

She didn't see Mike or Harry then or when she returned the dog to Sword of the King's stall. But she did see them outside the track, climbing into an old car that was parked near hers. Their car was covered with dust, and there were clothes in the back seat.

Of course, Rita said to herself. She had not thought they were from around there.

3

The next day Rita Green got to the racetrack at the same time she always did. Right away, she knew something was wrong. She saw Mr. Boynton's car parked near the new stable building with its engine running. Owners could drive near the stables, but Mr. Boynton almost never did. He left his car outside the track most days.

Mr. Boynton was standing outside Sword of the King's stall. "What are you doing here so early?" Mr. Boynton asked.

"I came in early so I could take Sparky for his morning walk."

"Sparky isn't here."

"But . . . where is he?"

"I don't know." Mr. Boynton looked angry, but he didn't seem to be worrying. "Maybe he took it into his head to run off." Then the horse's owner stopped talking. He just stood there, watching Rita.

"No." Rita shook her head. "He wouldn't do that."

"Why not?"

Rita didn't like the way Mr. Boynton was looking at her. "I don't know. He just wouldn't. He always stays near Sword of the King. The only time he leaves is when I take him for a walk."

"Well, he is gone now," Mr. Boynton said. "What do you think happened? Where do you think he is?"

Rita made a face. "I don't know." She didn't like the way Mr. Boynton kept looking at her. She had not done anything wrong, but the man made her feel as though she had.

"Are you sure you didn't take Sparky home with you?" the owner asked.

"I wouldn't do that," Rita said.

"Why not? You like the dog, don't you?"

"Yes, I like him fine, but—"

"But?"

"But he does not belong to me," Rita said.

Sword of the King hit the inside of the stall a few times with his foot. It sounded like a gun going off. Mr. Boynton just looked at Rita for a while without saying anything. Then he said, "I want you to look for that dog. And find him. I want him back here."

"Yes, Mr. Boynton," Rita said. "Whatever you want."

"Good." Sword of the King's owner looked at her again and then walked away.

Every other time Rita had talked to the man, he had been all smiles. But not this time. So Rita knew the dog was important to him for some reason. She wondered what it was.

Rita opened the lower half of the stall door. She wanted to get Sparky's rope. If she found the dog, she thought she might need it. She reached inside, but the rope was gone.

4

Rita Green looked for Sparky all morning. She walked all around the track many times, looking every place she thought the dog might go. And she asked everyone she met if they had seen the dog. No one had.

Mr. Boynton had not seemed to be worrying, but now Rita was. Sparky was not the kind of dog who runs away. And his rope was gone, too. That made it look as though someone had taken him. Someone may have tied him with his rope and led him away.

But why? He was just a little dog who slept in Sword of the King's stall. He wasn't worth anything. No one would pay money for him. There were hundreds of little dogs like him in any city. Why would anyone take him? It didn't add up.

At noon, Rita returned to the stable. Mr. Boynton was there with Sword of the King's trainer. Rita got there just in time to hear the trainer say the horse wasn't running well. "His time around the track was poor," he said. Then they saw Rita.

"Did you find the dog?" Mr. Boynton asked.

"No, I didn't. I looked everywhere, but he isn't around the track."

The owner made a face.

"Should I keep looking?" Rita asked.

"Keep looking?" he said as though Rita was crazy. "Of course you should keep looking! Don't do anything else. Find that dog. And if you don't find him by Monday, don't bother to come back." He almost shouted the words, he was so angry. Then he turned and walked out of the stable without looking back.

"Why is he mad at me?" Rita asked the trainer.

"He has been looking for the dog, too," the man said. "He asked around. You are the last one who was seen with Sparky. He knows you liked that dog and he thinks you took him."

"But I didn't," Rita said.

The trainer smiled at her, trying to be kind. "Then you have a problem," he said.

"Yes, I guess I do. But I don't know why. Why should he make such a big thing out of a missing dog?"

"It isn't the dog he is worrying about—it is Sword of the King."

Rita was lost now. "What are you saying?"

"I'm saying, Sword of the King isn't running as fast as he did before. He does not look as though he slept at all last night. He misses his little friend and wants him back. So that is what Mr. Boynton wants, too. If he does not run his best, Sword of the King won't win the big race on Monday."

Then Rita heard the noise from Sword of the King's stall. The big horse moved around and hit the walls over and over. He seemed angry about something. Maybe they were right. Maybe he did miss his little friend. Rita had never heard so much noise from his stall before.

"What do you think I should do?" Rita asked the trainer.

The man held out his hands and shook his head. Then he said, "There is only one thing you can do."

"What?"

"Find Sparky."

"But I have looked everywhere."

"Not everywhere. There is one place you have not looked."

"Where is that?"

"The dog must be somewhere. So you have not looked in the right place."

"Thanks. You are a big help," Rita said in a quiet voice. "That leaves me the whole world to look in."

"Glad to be of help," the trainer said, all smiles.

5

Rita went out to her car and sat thinking for a long time. She knew much more now than she did at the start, but she needed to know more. Sparky could have run off by himself, but Rita did not think he had. The missing rope made it look like someone had taken the dog.

But who? And why? Maybe if she knew why, she would have no trouble guessing who. Maybe . . .

She sat and thought about that for a while.

Maybe someone had known Sword of the King would not run his best if the little black dog was gone. Maybe one of the other owners wanted to give his own horse a better chance to win the big race. But no, she didn't think any of them would do that to win.

So who else might want Sword of the King not to run so fast? And again, why? If she knew the answer to that, maybe she would know who. And if she knew who, maybe she could get the dog back and save her job.

She sat, trying to think. Had she seen any changes now that the dog was gone? No, everything was the same. Then she thought of Mike and Harry. They had not been around. Any other day, she would have seen them three or four times. But she had been all around the track many times and had not seen them even once. That was strange.

Would Mike and Harry have wanted to make Sword of the King slow down? What would they get out of that? They had been trying to find out which horse had the most speed. But wait—that was not true. It just seemed that way. They had not wanted to know which horse had the most speed—they wanted to know which horse would win the big race. That was not the same thing at all.

Rita gave it some more thought. Suddenly, she had it. If they were sure Sword of the King would not win the big race, that might be all they would need. Most people would still bet on him. They could bet on all the other horses in the race and still make money. That was the answer. Rita was sure of it.

Rita climbed out of her car and walked back to the track. For the first time in the hours that Sparky had been gone, she didn't feel like she was walking around in the dark. A light had been turned on. Now she knew what she had to do. She had to find Mike and Harry. And to do that, she had to know more about them.

6

Rita stopped to talk to the man at the gate. Mike and Harry had parked their car near hers, so Rita thought they probably used the same gate she did.

"Have you seen Mike and Harry today?" Rita asked.

"Who?" the man asked.

"Mike and Harry."

"Don't know them."

"Two men, one thin and the other big and round. The heavy one is called Harry," Rita said, telling him what they looked like.

"No, they don't use this gate," the man said. "I have never seen them."

There were two other gates they might have used. Rita went to the first one and then to the other. She asked the same questions and got the same answers. The men at the gates didn't know Mike and Harry. And they didn't remember ever seeing them.

Rita had not thought they belonged back by the stables. Now she was sure of it. They could not have entered at one of the gates without showing their stable passes. And they would have been remembered. Now Rita knew they must have climbed the fence to get in or slipped in some other way.

She asked around inside, but no one had seen Mike or Harry. Now Rita was more sure than ever that she was on the right track. Mike and Harry had always been around before. But now that Sparky was gone, so were they.

She still could not be sure they had the dog, but it looked that way. To be sure, she would have to find them.

She went back to her car and sat behind

the wheel. What was her next move? Where did she go from here? The city was far too large for her to drive up and down the streets, looking for their car. Besides, there was not enough time for that. She had to find Sparky before the big race on Monday.

But what if she found them and they did not have the dog? What would she do then? Rita shook her head to clear it. She would worry about that if and when it happened. Finding Mike and Harry was the only problem she could take care of right now. And maybe she could not do that.

She had hoped to find out more about them, but she had not. That left her with nothing but the little she had known. She had only seen them the last few weeks. That seemed to say they were new, probably just moved to the city. And their car was covered with road dirt and had clothes in the back seat. They showed pretty much the same thing. They had not seemed to be the kind of men who would stay anywhere for very long. They had seemed to have their eyes on the big race and nothing else. They were probably going to move on when it was over.

That wasn't very much to go on. It was almost nothing. Rita wanted to add it all up and somehow find her next move. Her mother had always told her she was good at adding two and two and ending up with five. This was the test that would show if she was right.

What would men like that do when they came to a new city? Would they find a house somewhere? No, that didn't seem right. Houses were for people who were going to stay a while. A room then? That was more like it. They would rent a room. But where and what kind?

She was sure they wanted to bet on the big race. So they would want to have as much money for that as they could. They would want a room that didn't cost too much.

All right, but where? She turned her thoughts to that. If they had had to drive a long time to reach the city, they wouldn't feel like spending much time looking for a room. Rita knew that in their place she would not. They would probably take one of the first ones they found.

Rita smiled to herself and started the engine. Now she knew where to look for them.

7

Rita drove down the road. Every time she saw a place that rented rooms, she pulled in and looked for their car. She didn't see it.

There were a few dirt-covered old cars parked, but not one of them was the one she was looking for. Maybe this wasn't going to be as easy as she had thought.

When she was well outside the city, she turned around and headed back. This time she didn't just look for their car. This time she stopped to ask a few questions. She didn't tell anyone their names were Mike and Harry because she was no longer sure those were their right names. But she told everyone what they looked like as well as she could.

After she had been to ten places, Rita still had not found anyone who knew them. Her high hopes were starting to slip away by the time she got to the next place. But here the man behind the desk listened to what Rita had to say.

"You must be talking about Mike and Harry," he said.

It was as though the sun had come out and happy music was playing. "That is right," Rita said. "What room are they staying in?"

"No room," the man said. "They are not staying here anymore. I had to ask them to leave. Their dog kept everybody up all night. You never heard such noise."

"A dog?" Rita said. "What kind of a dog was it?"

"I don't know. Just a dog—a little black one."

Sparky! Rita thought.

The man said, "It wouldn't shut up, so I asked them to go."

"When was that?" Rita asked.

"This morning. As soon as people told me about all the noise last night. We don't let people bring dogs in here. If I had known they had a dog, I would not have rented them a room. I didn't see the dog when they came two weeks ago. They must have just got it."

"I think you are right," Rita said. "I think they just got the dog."

"They shouldn't have done that," the man said. "They should have known no one would want a loud dog around. People come here to sleep, not be kept up all night."

Rita said, "Look—can you guess where they went from here?"

"I don't know and I don't care," the man said. "I sure didn't ask."

8

Now Rita was sure Mike and Harry had Sparky, but she was worse off now than she had been before. It had just been her good luck that she had found where they were staying. But to find out they had moved was a real blow. She might never find them again. They probably weren't in any hurry when they looked for their new room. They could have gone anywhere in the city.

But Rita didn't have the time to look everywhere. And she could not stop looking. She had to keep trying to find them. Mr. Boynton wanted Sparky back. And Rita didn't want her job lost over this if she could help it.

Because she didn't have a better plan, she kept doing the same thing she had been doing. She climbed back into her car and stayed on the same road. There was a chance that Mike and Harry had done that too. She stopped and asked questions whenever she saw a sign about rooms for rent. After dark she got very hungry, but she kept going for two more hours. Then she stopped to eat at a McDonald's before going on down the road.

At ten o'clock she saw that she was near the racetrack. There were many places around there that rented rooms or cabins. Now she didn't know what to do. Would they bring the dog to a place so near the track? If not, maybe she should just pass these places by. Maybe . . .

Because she could not make up her mind, she stopped at a place renting cabins anyway. She could see the racetrack from where she parked her car. That didn't seem like a very good sign. But she was wrong.

"Yes, they are here," the woman running the place told her. The woman had long black hair and a thin face. "They just checked in a few hours ago. One is heavy and the other thin—Mike and Harry, right?"

"Right. And they have a little black dog with them, don't they?" Rita said.

The woman gave Rita a strange look. "A dog? No, I didn't see any dog. Just Mike and Harry."

They probably hid the dog in their car until they had rented the room, Rita thought. The woman might not have rented them the room if she knew they had a dog.

"Where are they staying?" Rita asked.

"I gave them one of the cabins in back," she said, and told her which one.

Rita walked back. She was tired, but she was happy the hunt for Sparky was over.

A light was on in the cabin window, and their old car was parked in front. Rita was as quiet as she could be as she moved near the door. She put her ear against it. Everything was quiet inside. They didn't even have the TV on.

Then she heard Mike's voice come from the other side of the door. "That dog will wake up soon, won't he?"

"Yes," Harry answered. "I don't have any more sleeping pills to give him."

"If he wakes up and starts to make noise, I'm going to kill him," Mike said.

9

Rita backed away from the door. Her mind raced. What should she do? What could she do? It was clear to her that Mike and Harry had Sparky in their cabin. The dog had been given sleeping pills to keep him quiet. But Mike had said he would kill him if the dog should wake up and make noise. And he might wake up at any time. Rita knew the little dog too well to think there was any chance he would wake up and be quiet.

Rita also knew she wouldn't have a chance against the two men. She had to think of something. Better still, she had to get help. There had to be someone who would help her.

Suddenly, she had the answer. She ran to where she had parked her car in front of the office. There was an outdoor telephone on the wall of the office. A telephone book was beside it.

First, she called the track. It was late, but someone must be around. The phone rang eight times, but no one answered. She called again, thinking she might have got the number wrong. Still no answer.

Now what? The telephone book! She opened it and began looking for Mr. Boynton's number. She called that number and the telephone was answered by a woman.

"Mr. Boynton, please," Rita said. "Rita Green calling."

"I'm sorry," she said. "This is Mrs. Boynton. My husband isn't home."

"Not home?" Rita said. What should she do now? "When will he be back?" she asked.

"I'm not sure," Mrs. Boynton said. "Do you want me to tell him anything when he comes in?"

"Yes, I do," Rita said. "Please tell him I found out where Sparky is. Two men have him in a rented cabin." She went on to tell Mrs. Boynton where and the cabin number. "I'll wait for him in front of the cabin until he can get here."

She got back to the cabin just as the door opened. Rita just had time to duck into the dark.

10

Mike stood there with the light from the room behind him. He had turned back to talk to Harry, and he was angry. "What? You won't let me kill that dog? Are you crazy?"

"He is a nice little dog, and I don't want you to hurt him," Harry said.

"You must be crazy," Mike said. "We are much nearer to the track than we were the other night. If he makes any noise, someone is sure to know where he came from."

"I don't care," Harry said. "I like him."

"Will you still like him if he brings the police down on us?"

Harry didn't answer.

"I didn't think so," Mike said. He walked back inside and shut the door behind him.

Rita moved to the door so she could listen. The men were still fighting, but it was clear that Mike was going to have his way.

Finally, Mike said, "I don't think I want to wait for him to wake up. We should do it while the dog is still sleeping. Get him, and carry him out to our car."

Rita was standing with her ear against the door. Suddenly it opened, and Rita almost fell into the cabin. The ear that had been against the door was now held by Mike, who used it to pull her the rest of the way into the room.

"Well, well!" Mike said to Rita. "You are a long way from home."

Rita did her best to get away, but Mike held on to her ear and then pushed her against the wall. "Not so fast," he said. "My friend and I want to talk to you. How did you find us?"

"I used my nose," Rita said. "You two smell bad."

"Laugh if you want to," Mike said, pulling a gun out of his pocket. "I wonder how much laughing you will do when I blow your head off with this."

Harry spoke up. "Wait a minute. I didn't bargain for this. Killing a dog is bad enough, but—"

"She brought it on herself," Mike said. "We didn't ask her to stick her nose in here, did we? What happens to her will be all her own doing."

"Well, maybe . . . "

Rita didn't like how this was going. It was easy for Mike to get Harry to think his way. She listened. She hoped she would hear cars or Mr. Boynton's running feet—anything that would tell her help was on the way. All she heard was Mike's voice and the beating of her own heart.

Finally, Mike said, "Enough talk. Let's all take a little ride." He pulled Rita's arm and then pushed her toward the door. Harry followed with the sleeping dog in his arms.

But when Mike opened the door, Mr.

Boynton was standing there with two policemen. Mike took one look at the policemen's guns and let go of his own. And as quickly as that, it was all over.

While the policemen took Mike and Harry away, Mr. Boynton turned to Rita. "You could have been killed," he said. "What made you take a chance like that?"

"I wanted to keep my job," Rita told him.

Mr. Boynton smiled and put his hand on Rita's arm. "Don't worry about that," he said. "You have a job with me as long as you want one."